INDIANA JONES

AND THE
SARGASSO PIRATES
PART 3

STORY
KARL KESEL

PENCIL BREAKDOWNS
KARL KESEL

INKS & FINISHES
EDUARDO BARRETO

COLORS
BERNIE MIREAULT

LETTERS
PAT BROSSEAU

COVER ART
RUSSELL WALKS

Spotlight

DARK HORSE COMICS

VISIT US AT
www.abdopublishing.com

Reinforced library bound edition published in 2011 by Spotlight, a division of the ABDO Group, 8000 West 78th Street, Edina, Minnesota 55439. Spotlight produces high-quality reinforced library bound editions for schools and libraries. Published by agreement with Dark Horse Comics, Inc., and Lucasfilm Ltd.

Printed in the United States of America, Melrose Park, Illinois.
052010
092010
 This book contains at least 10% recycled materials.

Library of Congress Cataloging-in-Publication Data

Kesel, Karl.
  Indiana Jones and the Sargasso pirates / script [by] Karl Kesel ; art [by] Eduardo Barreto.
      p. cm. -- (Indiana Jones and the Sargasso pirates ; 4)
  Summary: When Indiana Jones signs on with a band of pirates, he does not realize that his old nemesis is among them.
  ISBN 978-1-59961-761-9 (volume 1) -- ISBN 978-1-59961-762-6 (volume 2) -- ISBN 978-1-59961-763-3 (volume 3) -- ISBN 978-1-59961-764-0 (volume 4)
  1. Graphic novels. [1. Graphic novels. 2. Adventure and adventurers--Fiction. 3. Pirates--Fiction. 4. Sea stories.] I. Barreto, Eduardo, ill. II. Title.
  PZ7.7.K47 2011
  741.5'973--dc22
                                                            2010006485

All Spotlight books have reinforced library bindings and
are manufactured in the United States of America.

COULDN'TA BEEN BETTER IF'N I *PLANNED* IT...

ZACK -- MIND NO ONE *SPIES* YA, BUT DROPS THE WITCH'S CARCASS SOMEPLACE *WET* SO'S SHE AIN'T FOUND RIGHT QUICK.

I WANTS THE *EELS* TA WORK ON 'ER SOME.

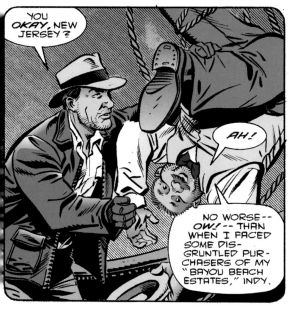

YOU *OKAY*, NEW JERSEY?

AH!

NO WORSE -- *OW!* -- THAN WHEN I FACED SOME DIS-GRUNTLED PUR-CHASERS OF MY "*BAYOU BEACH ESTATES*," INDY.

KEEP AN EYE ON *LAWTON.*

I'VE GOTTA FIND *SEGAR.* HE'S SECOND-IN-COMMAND -- SOME-ONE'S GOTTA TELL HIM WHAT HAPPENED TO THE *SEA WITCH*...

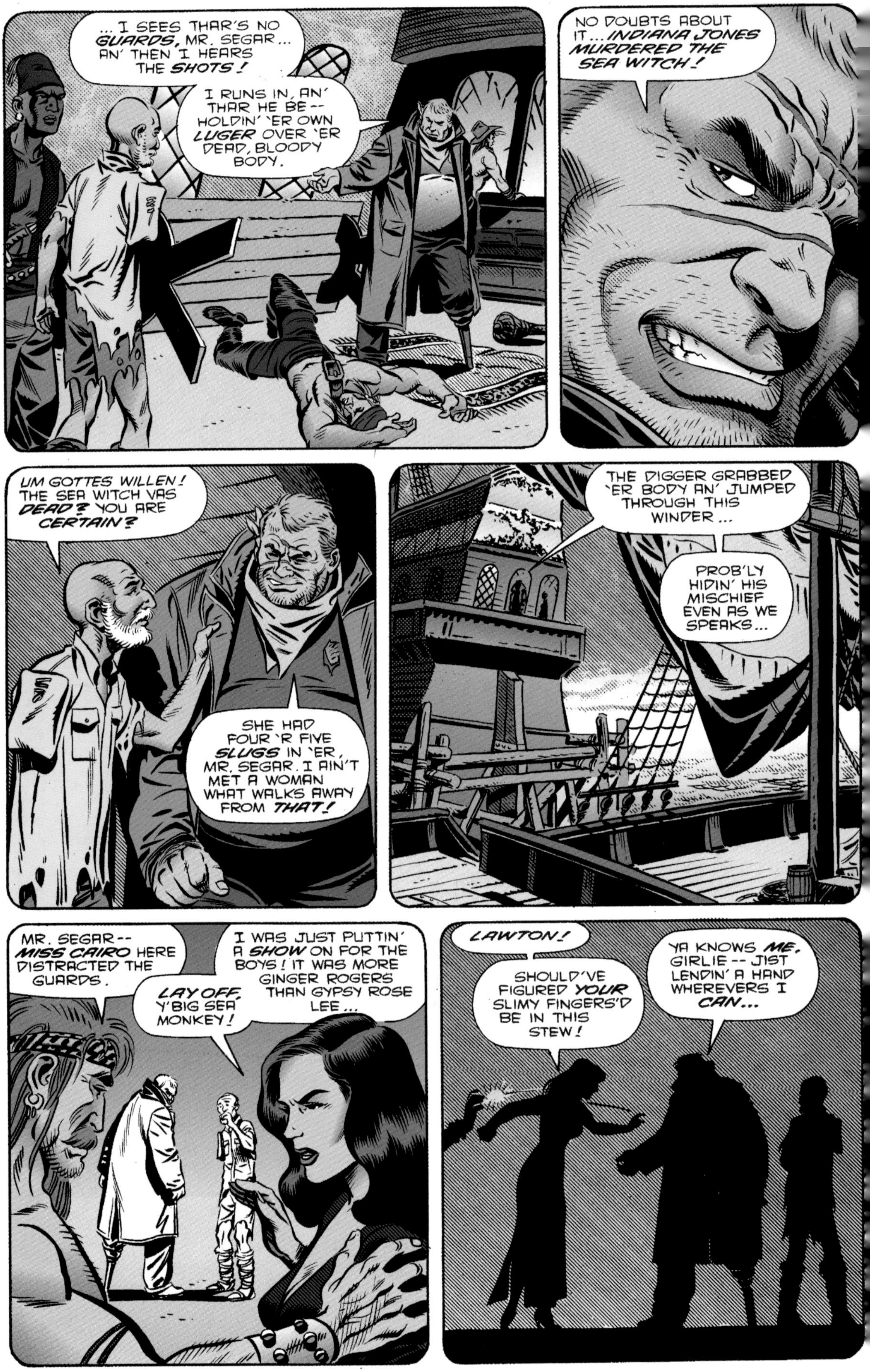
...I SEES THAR'S NO GUARDS, MR. SEGAR... AN' THEN I HEARS THE SHOTS!
I RUNS IN, AN' THAR HE BE -- HOLDIN' 'ER OWN LUGER OVER 'ER DEAD, BLOODY BODY.
NO DOUBTS ABOUT IT... INDIANA JONES MURDERED THE SEA WITCH!
UM GOTTES WILLEN! THE SEA WITCH VAS DEAD? YOU ARE CERTAIN?
SHE HAD FOUR 'R FIVE SLUGS IN 'ER, MR. SEGAR. I AIN'T MET A WOMAN WHAT WALKS AWAY FROM THAT!
THE DIGGER GRABBED 'ER BODY AN' JUMPED THROUGH THIS WINDER...
PROB'LY HIDIN' HIS MISCHIEF EVEN AS WE SPEAKS...
MR. SEGAR -- MISS CAIRO HERE DISTRACTED THE GUARDS.
I WAS JUST PUTTIN' A SHOW ON FOR THE BOYS! IT WAS MORE GINGER ROGERS THAN GYPSY ROSE LEE...
LAY OFF, Y'BIG SEA MONKEY!
LAWTON!
SHOULD'VE FIGURED YOUR SLIMY FINGERS'D BE IN THIS STEW!
YA KNOWS ME, GIRLIE -- JIST LENDIN' A HAND WHEREVERS I CAN...

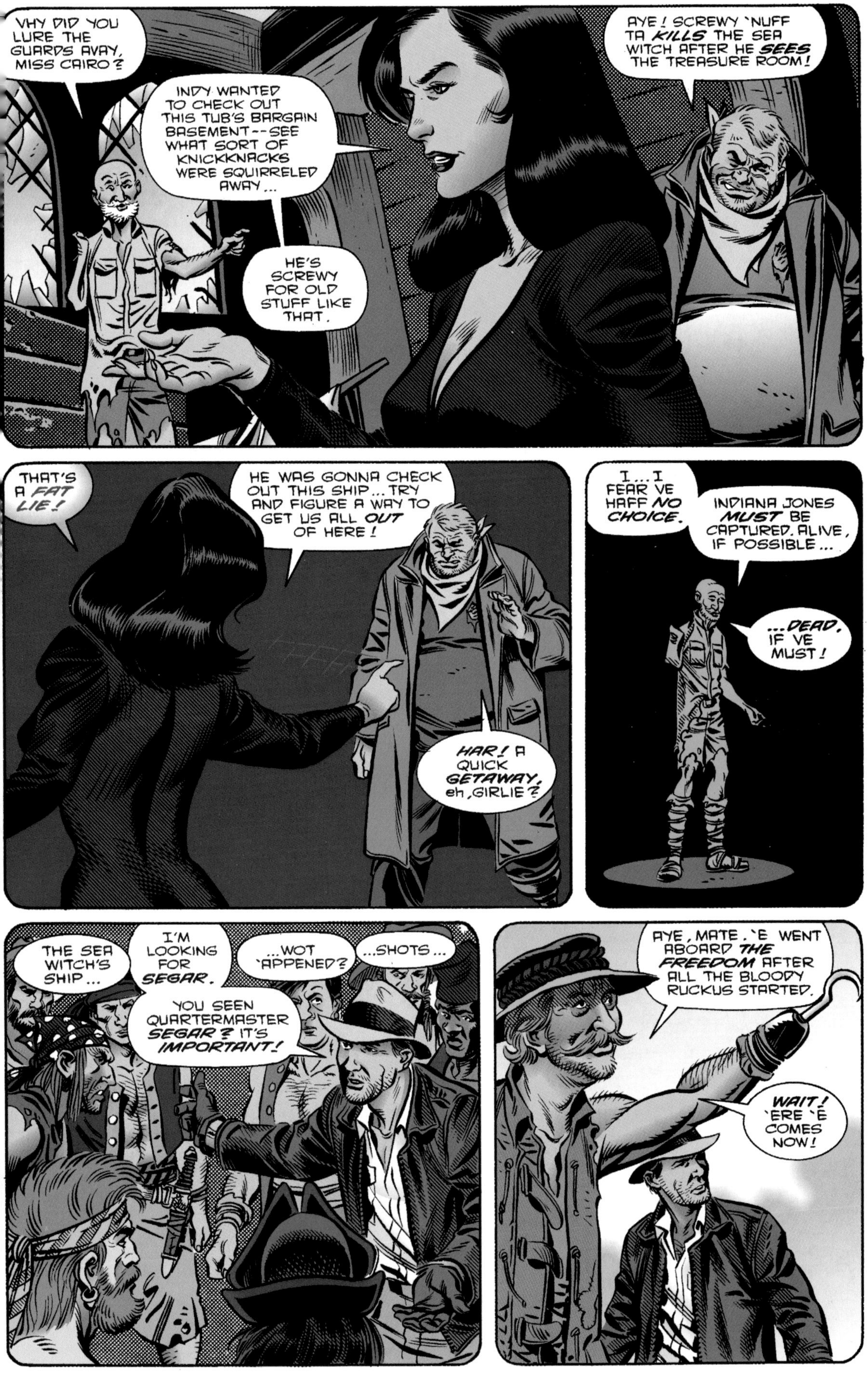
VHY DID YOU LURE THE GUARDS AVAY, MISS CAIRO?
INDY WANTED TO CHECK OUT THIS TUB'S BARGAIN BASEMENT--SEE WHAT SORT OF KNICKKNACKS WERE SQUIRRELED AWAY...
HE'S SCREWY FOR OLD STUFF LIKE THAT.
AYE! SCREWY 'NUFF TA KILLS THE SEA WITCH AFTER HE SEES THE TREASURE ROOM!
THAT'S A FAT LIE!
HE WAS GONNA CHECK OUT THIS SHIP... TRY AND FIGURE A WAY TO GET US ALL OUT OF HERE!
HAR! A QUICK GETAWAY, eh, GIRLIE?
I... I FEAR VE HAFF NO CHOICE.
INDIANA JONES MUST BE CAPTURED. ALIVE, IF POSSIBLE...
...DEAD, IF VE MUST!
THE SEA WITCH'S SHIP...
I'M LOOKING FOR SEGAR.
...WOT 'APPENED?
...SHOTS...
YOU SEEN QUARTERMASTER SEGAR? IT'S IMPORTANT!
AYE, MATE. 'E WENT ABOARD THE FREEDOM AFTER ALL THE BLOODY RUCKUS STARTED.
WAIT! 'ERE 'E COMES NOW!

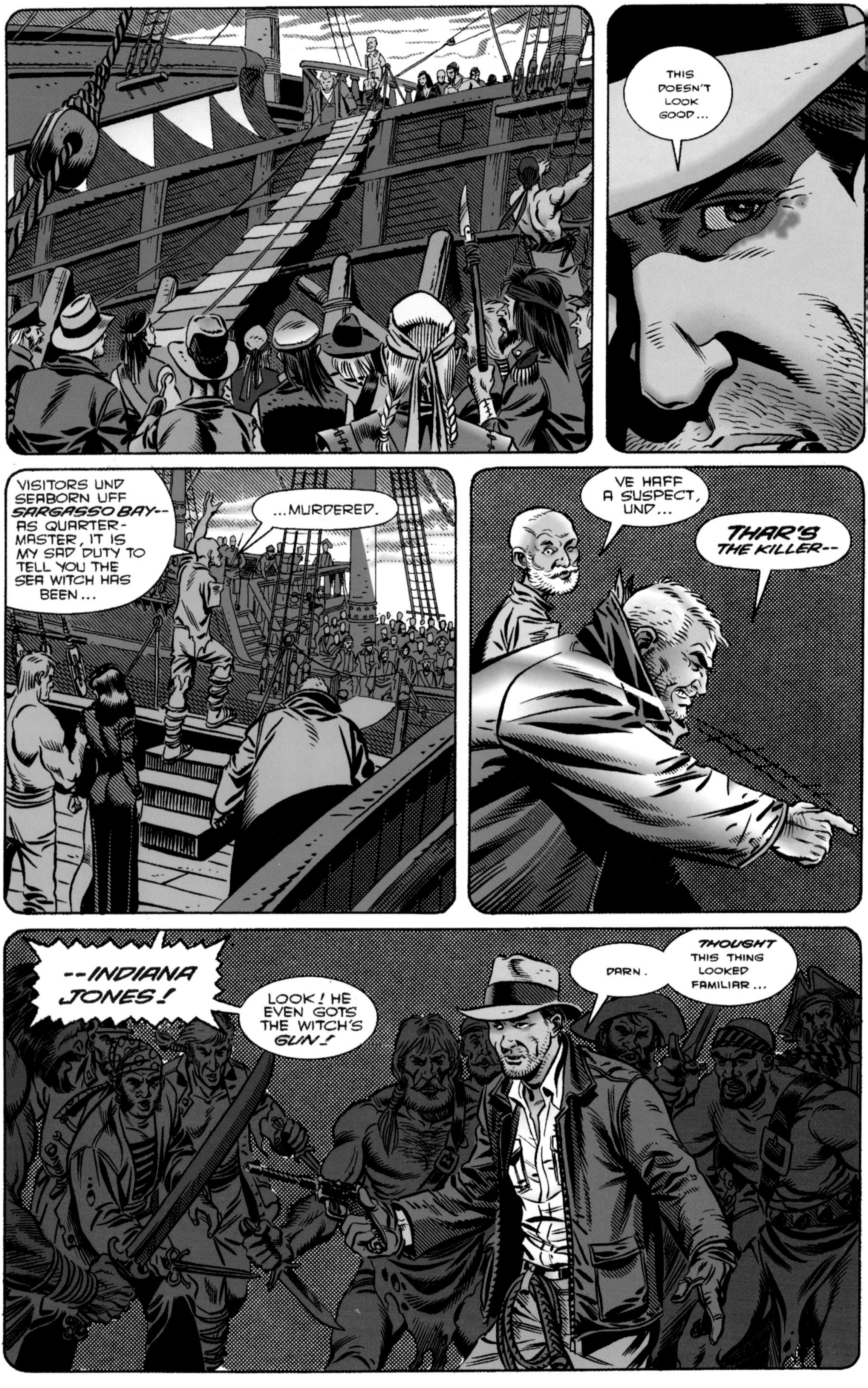
THIS DOESN'T LOOK GOOD...
VISITORS UND SEABORN UFF SARGASSO BAY-- AS QUARTER-MASTER, IT IS MY SAD DUTY TO TELL YOU THE SEA WITCH HAS BEEN...
...MURDERED.
VE HAFF A SUSPECT, UND...
THAR'S THE KILLER--
--INDIANA JONES!
LOOK! HE EVEN GOTS THE WITCH'S GUN!
DARN.
THOUGHT THIS THING LOOKED FAMILIAR...

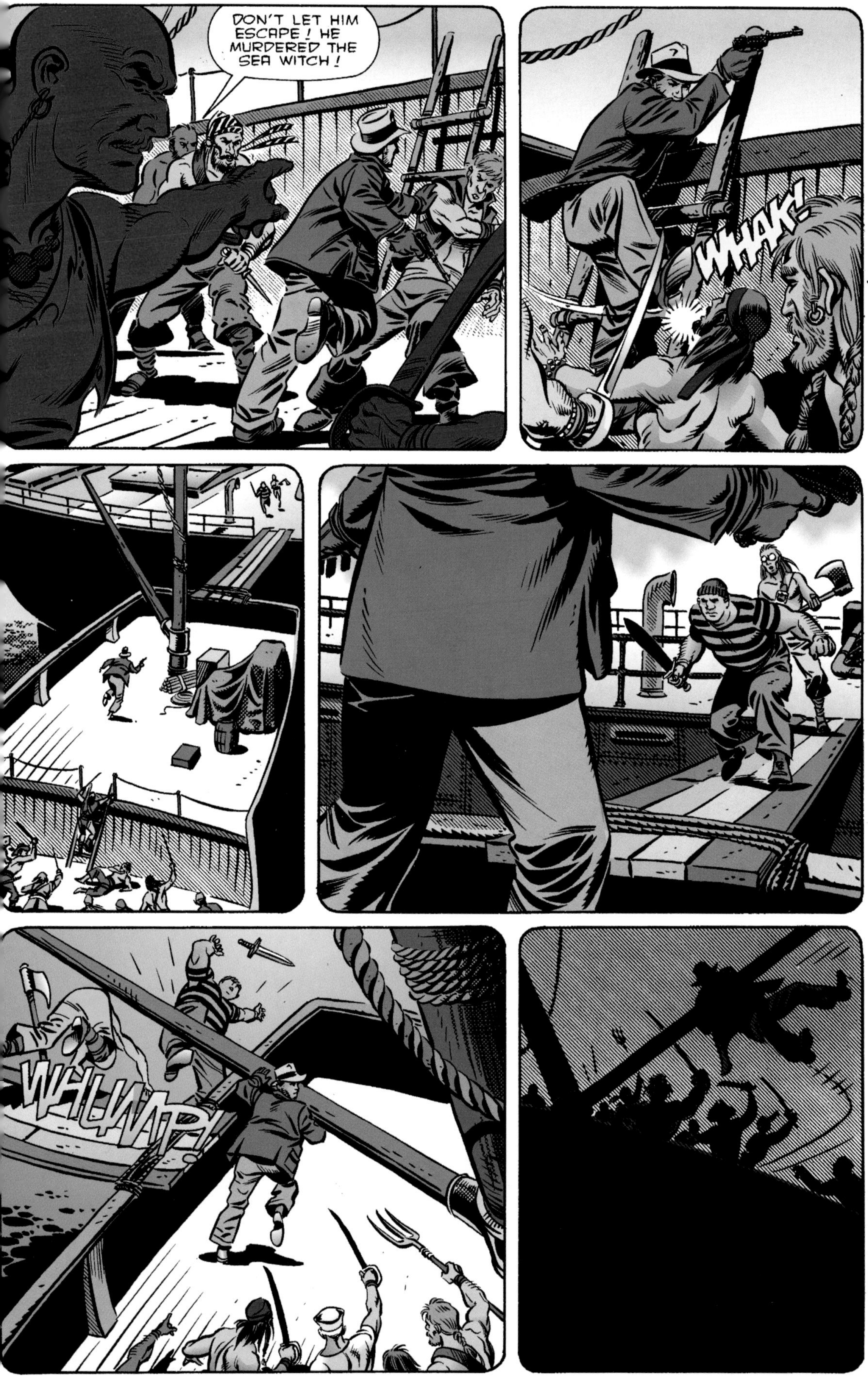
DON'T LET HIM ESCAPE! HE MURDERED THE SEA WITCH!
WHAK!
WHUMP!

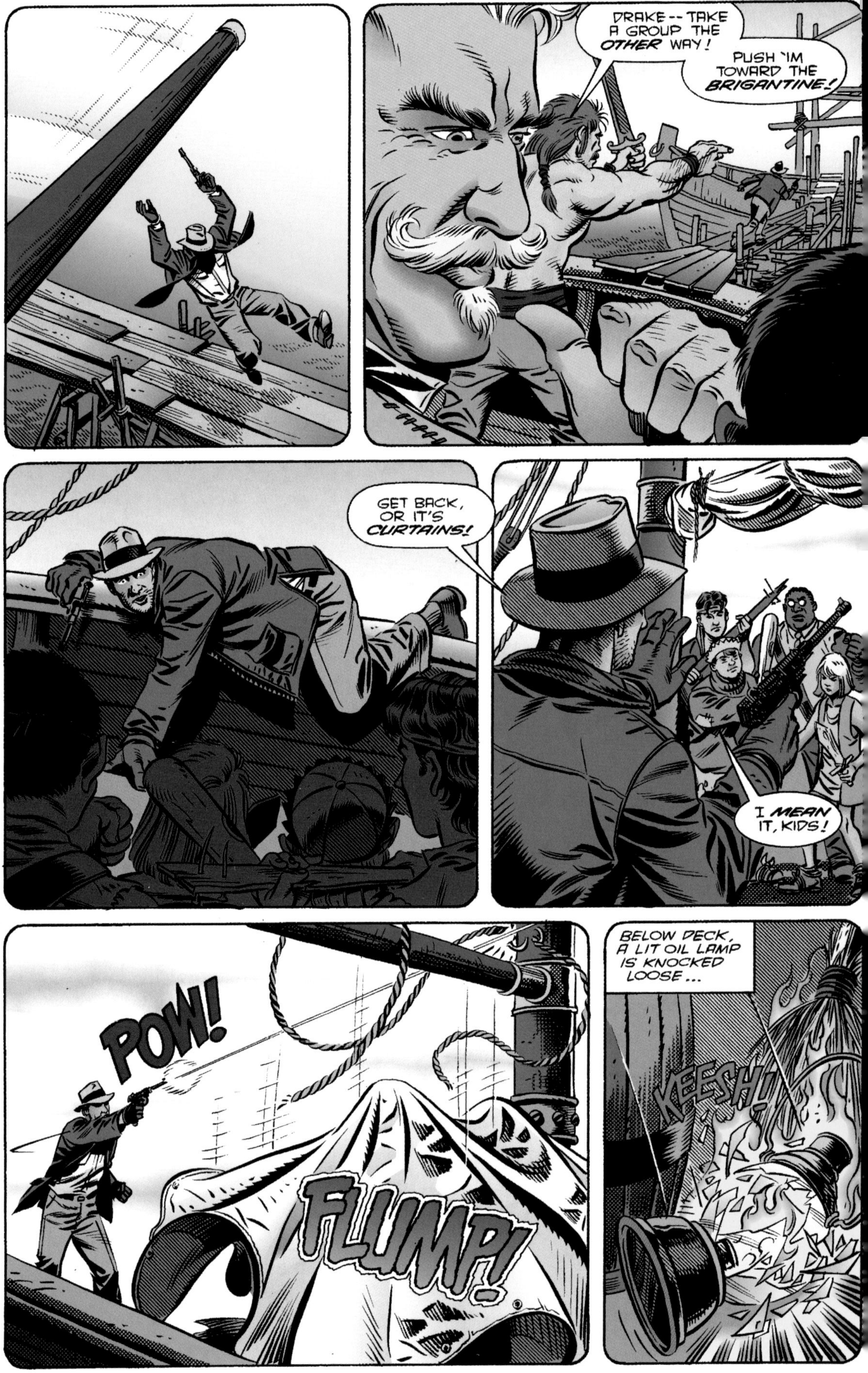
DRAKE -- TAKE A GROUP THE OTHER WAY!
PUSH 'IM TOWARD THE BRIGANTINE!
GET BACK, OR IT'S CURTAINS!
I MEAN IT, KIDS!
POW!
FLUMP!
BELOW DECK, A LIT OIL LAMP IS KNOCKED LOOSE...
KEESH!

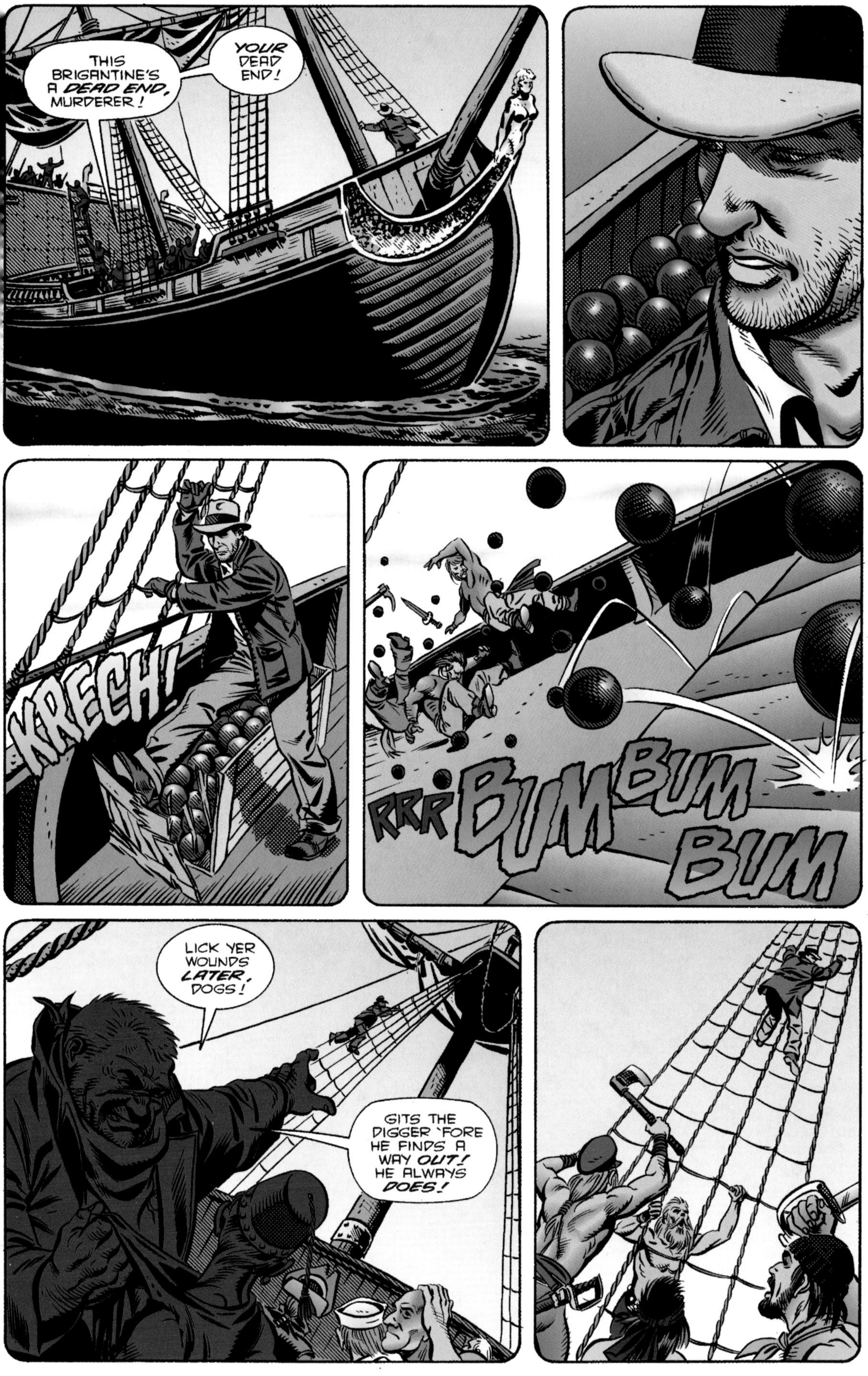
THIS BRIGANTINE'S A DEAD END, MURDERER!
YOUR DEAD END!
KRECH!
RRRBUMBUMBUM BUM
LICK YER WOUNDS LATER, DOGS!
GITS THE DIGGER 'FORE HE FINDS A WAY OUT! HE ALWAYS DOES!

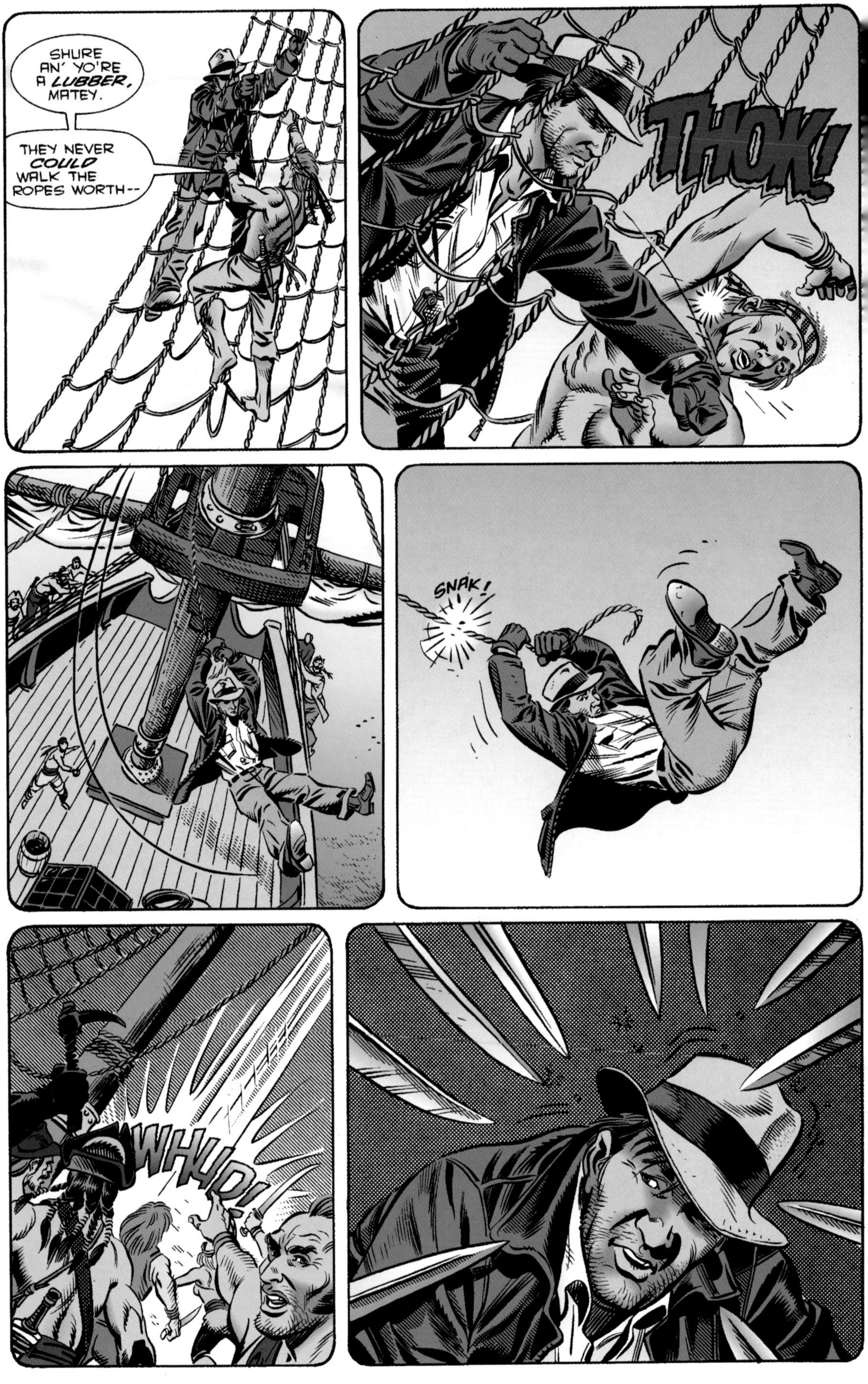
SHURE AN' YO'RE A LUBBER, MATEY.
THEY NEVER COULD WALK THE ROPES WORTH--
THOK!
SNAK!
WHUD!

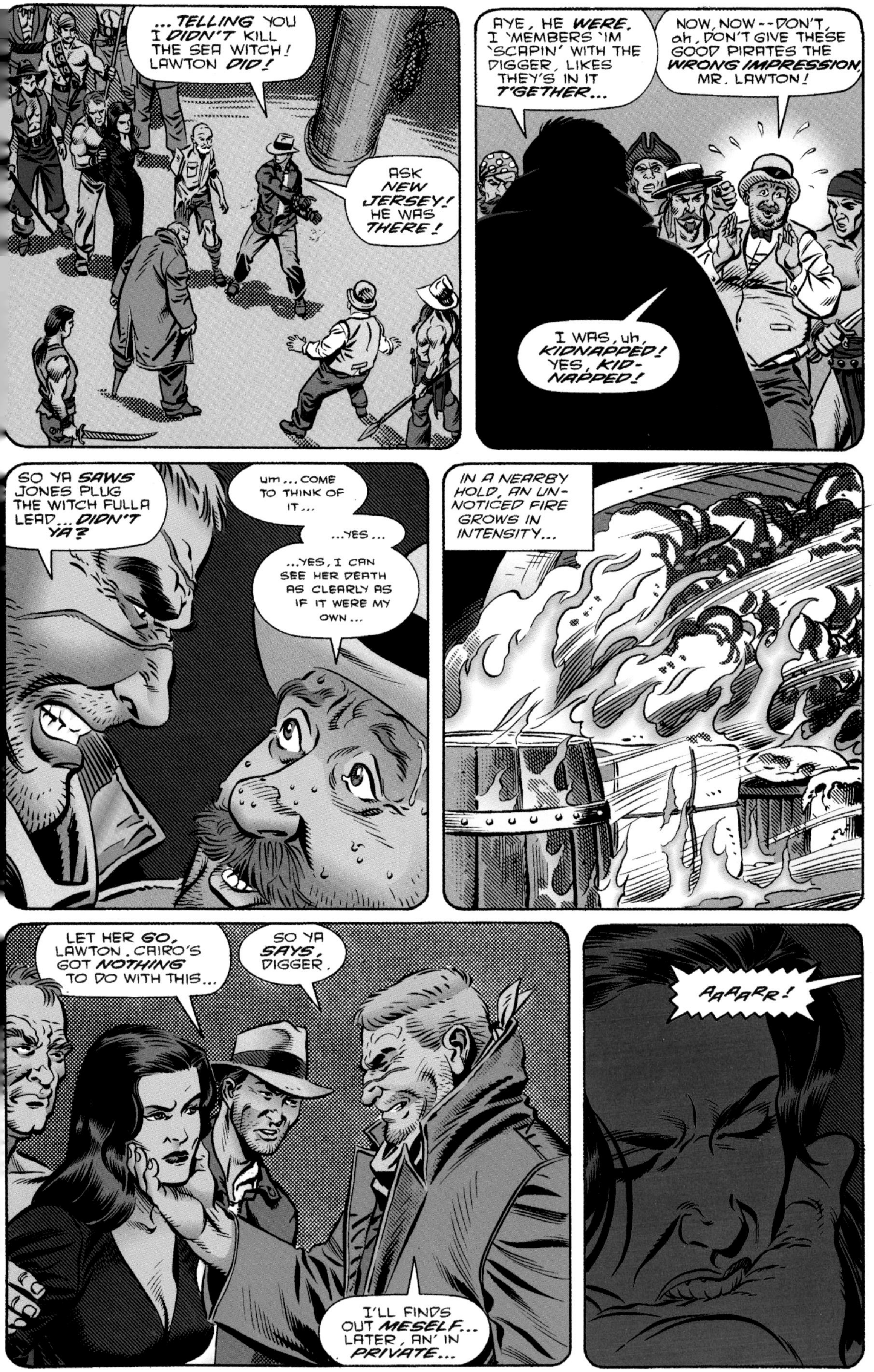
...TELLING YOU I DIDN'T KILL THE SEA WITCH! LAWTON DID!
ASK NEW JERSEY! HE WAS THERE!
AYE, HE WERE. I 'MEMBERS 'IM 'SCAPIN' WITH THE DIGGER, LIKES THEY'S IN IT T'GETHER...
NOW, NOW--DON'T, ah, DON'T GIVE THESE GOOD PIRATES THE WRONG IMPRESSION, MR. LAWTON!
I WAS, uh, KIDNAPPED! YES, KID-NAPPED!
SO YA SAWS JONES PLUG THE WITCH FULLA LEAD... DIDN'T YA?
um... COME TO THINK OF IT...
...YES...
...YES, I CAN SEE HER DEATH AS CLEARLY AS IF IT WERE MY OWN...
IN A NEARBY HOLD, AN UN-NOTICED FIRE GROWS IN INTENSITY...
LET HER GO, LAWTON. CAIRO'S GOT NOTHING TO DO WITH THIS...
SO YA SAYS, DIGGER.
I'LL FINDS OUT MESELF... LATER, AN' IN PRIVATE...
AAAARR!

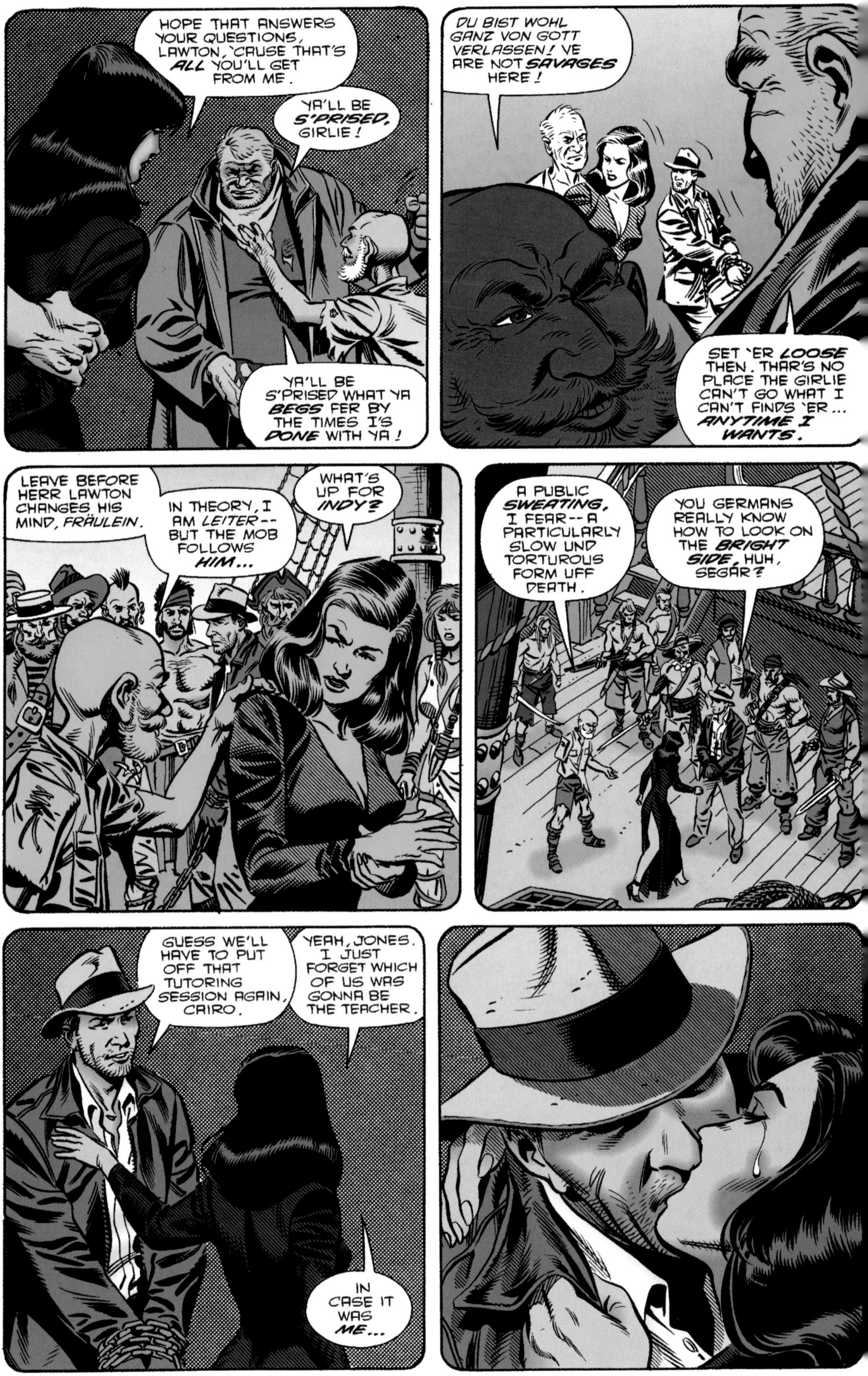
HOPE THAT ANSWERS YOUR QUESTIONS, LAWTON, 'CAUSE THAT'S *ALL* YOU'LL GET FROM ME.
YA'LL BE *S'PRISED,* GIRLIE!
YA'LL BE S'PRISED WHAT YA *BEGS* FER BY THE TIMES I'S *DONE* WITH YA!
DU BIST WOHL GANZ VON GOTT VERLASSEN! VE ARE NOT *SAVAGES* HERE!
SET 'ER *LOOSE* THEN. THAR'S NO PLACE THE GIRLIE CAN'T GO WHAT I CAN'T FINDS 'ER... *ANYTIME I WANTS.*
LEAVE BEFORE HERR LAWTON CHANGES HIS MIND, *FRÄULEIN.*
IN THEORY, I AM *LEITER*-- BUT THE MOB FOLLOWS *HIM*...
WHAT'S UP FOR *INDY?*
A PUBLIC *SWEATING,* I FEAR-- A PARTICULARLY SLOW UND TORTUROUS FORM UFF DEATH.
YOU GERMANS REALLY KNOW HOW TO LOOK ON THE *BRIGHT SIDE,* HUH, SEGAR?
GUESS WE'LL HAVE TO PUT OFF THAT TUTORING SESSION AGAIN, CAIRO.
YEAH, JONES. I JUST FORGET WHICH OF US WAS GONNA BE THE TEACHER.
IN CASE IT WAS *ME*...

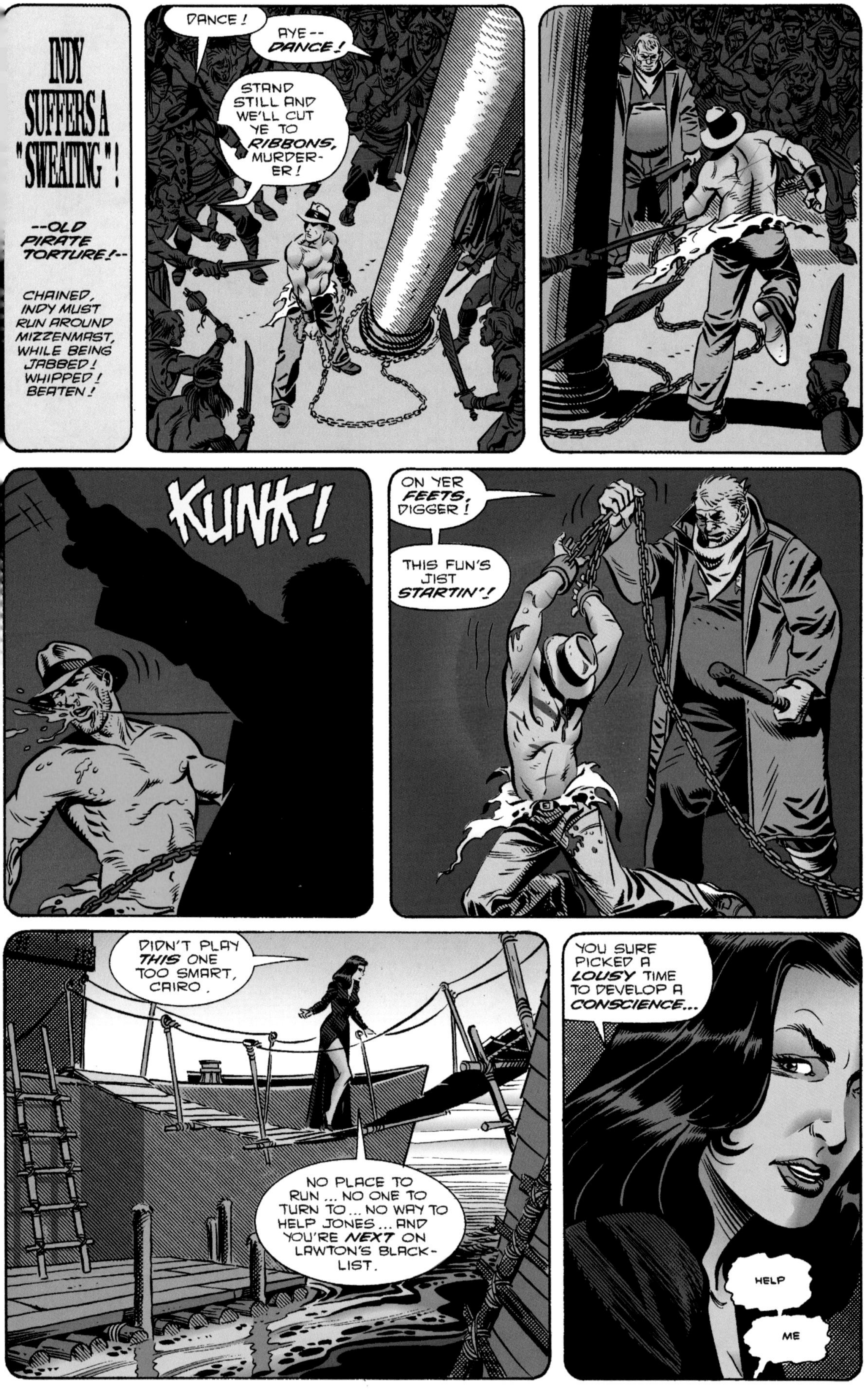
INDY SUFFERS A "SWEATING"!
--OLD PIRATE TORTURE!--
CHAINED, INDY MUST RUN AROUND MIZZENMAST, WHILE BEING JABBED! WHIPPED! BEATEN!
DANCE!
AYE-- DANCE!
STAND STILL AND WE'LL CUT YE TO RIBBONS, MURDERER!
KUNK!
ON YER FEETS, DIGGER!
THIS FUN'S JIST STARTIN'!
DIDN'T PLAY THIS ONE TOO SMART, CAIRO.
NO PLACE TO RUN ... NO ONE TO TURN TO ... NO WAY TO HELP JONES ... AND YOU'RE NEXT ON LAWTON'S BLACK-LIST.
YOU SURE PICKED A LOUSY TIME TO DEVELOP A CONSCIENCE...
HELP
ME

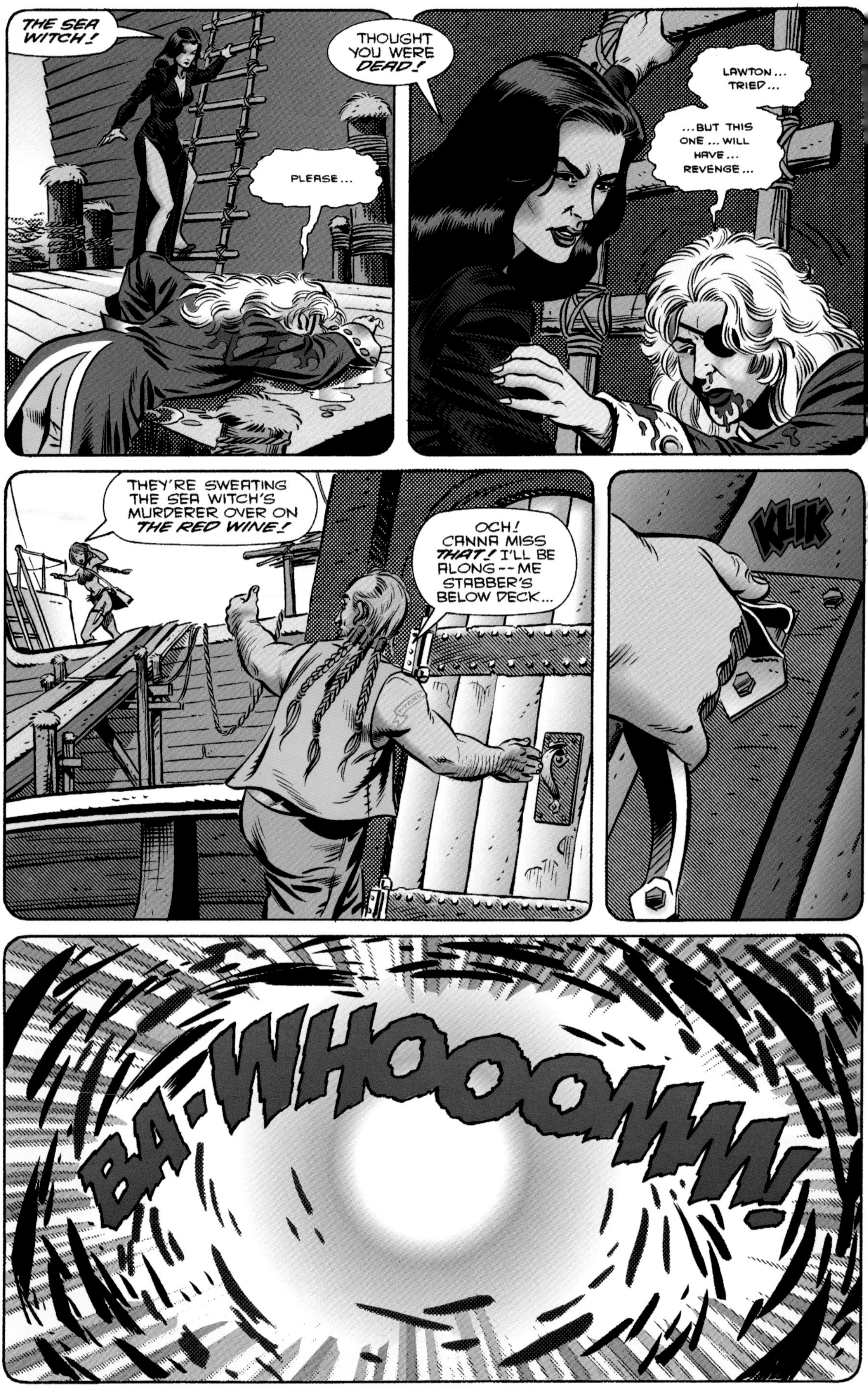
THE SEA WITCH!
PLEASE...
THOUGHT YOU WERE DEAD!
LAWTON... TRIED...
...BUT THIS ONE... WILL HAVE... REVENGE...
THEY'RE SWEATING THE SEA WITCH'S MURDERER OVER ON THE RED WINE!
OCH! CANNA MISS THAT! I'LL BE ALONG--ME STABBER'S BELOW DECK...
KLIK
BA-WHOOOM!

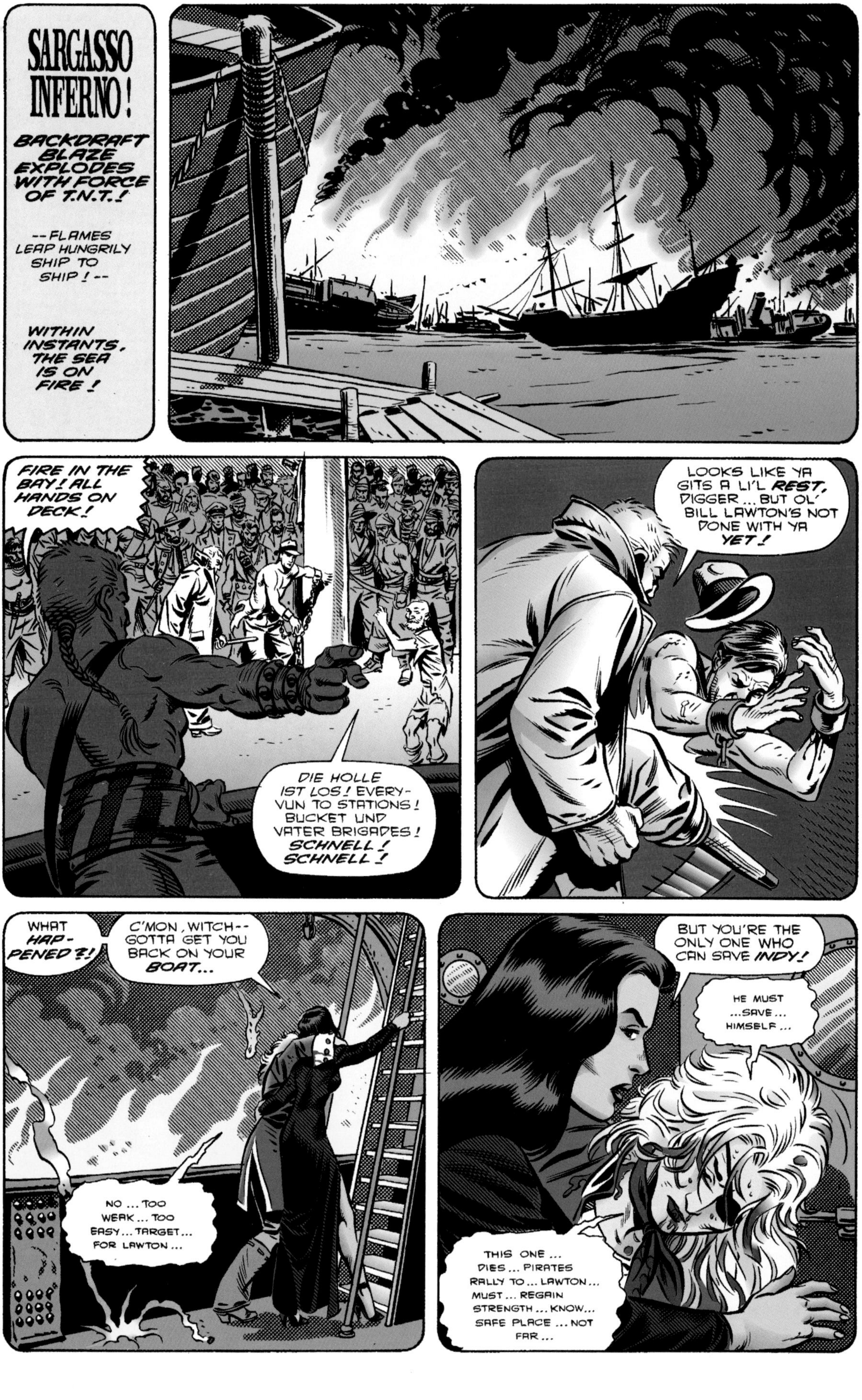
SARGASSO INFERNO!
BACKDRAFT BLAZE EXPLODES WITH FORCE OF T.N.T.!
--FLAMES LEAP HUNGRILY SHIP TO SHIP!--
WITHIN INSTANTS, THE SEA IS ON FIRE!
FIRE IN THE BAY! ALL HANDS ON DECK!
DIE HOLLE IST LOS! EVERY-VUN TO STATIONS! BUCKET UND VATER BRIGADES! SCHNELL! SCHNELL!
LOOKS LIKE YA GITS A LI'L REST, DIGGER... BUT OL' BILL LAWTON'S NOT DONE WITH YA YET!
WHAT HAP-PENED?!
C'MON, WITCH-- GOTTA GET YOU BACK ON YOUR BOAT...
NO... TOO WEAK... TOO EASY... TARGET... FOR LAWTON...
BUT YOU'RE THE ONLY ONE WHO CAN SAVE INDY!
HE MUST ...SAVE... HIMSELF...
THIS ONE... DIES... PIRATES RALLY TO... LAWTON... MUST... REGAIN STRENGTH... KNOW... SAFE PLACE... NOT FAR...

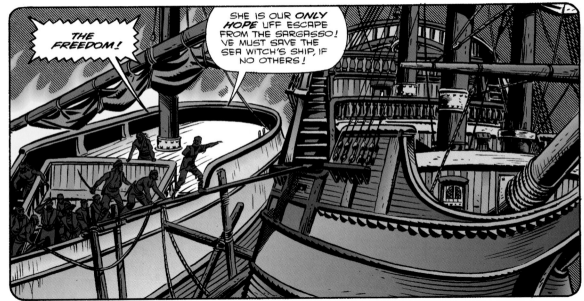

THE FREEDOM!

SHE IS OUR *ONLY HOPE* UFF ESCAPE FROM THE SARGASSO! VE MUST SAVE THE SEA WITCH'S SHIP, IF NO OTHERS!

...HERE WE ARE!

HEY -- SOME SWELL HIDEOUT YOU GOT HERE, SEA WITCH!

BELIEVE ME, I'VE SEEN MY SHARE.

PRETTY SHARP, FIXING UP THE HIDDEN ROOM IN THIS OLD RUMRUNNER IN CASE YOU HAD TO *LAM* IT.

ALWAYS PREPARED, HUH?

'COURSE, IN *YOUR* CASE, DON'T KNOW IF THAT MEANS YOU SHOULD'VE BEEN A *GIRL SCOUT* OR *HITLER YOUTH*.

MY MEN... MUSTN'T SEE ME... LIKE THIS... JONES...

MUSTN'T KNOW I... LONG FOR... MOUNTAINS... VALLEYS...

DOUBT *ANYONE* SAW US -- THEY'RE ALL FIGHTING THE *FIRE*.

WE SHOULD BE OKAY, THOUGH. THIS CRATE'S PRETTY FAR OUT.

JUST LET *NURSE CAIRO* DO HER STUFF.

LUCKY FOR YOU, I'VE HANDLED BULLET WOUNDS *BE-FORE*...

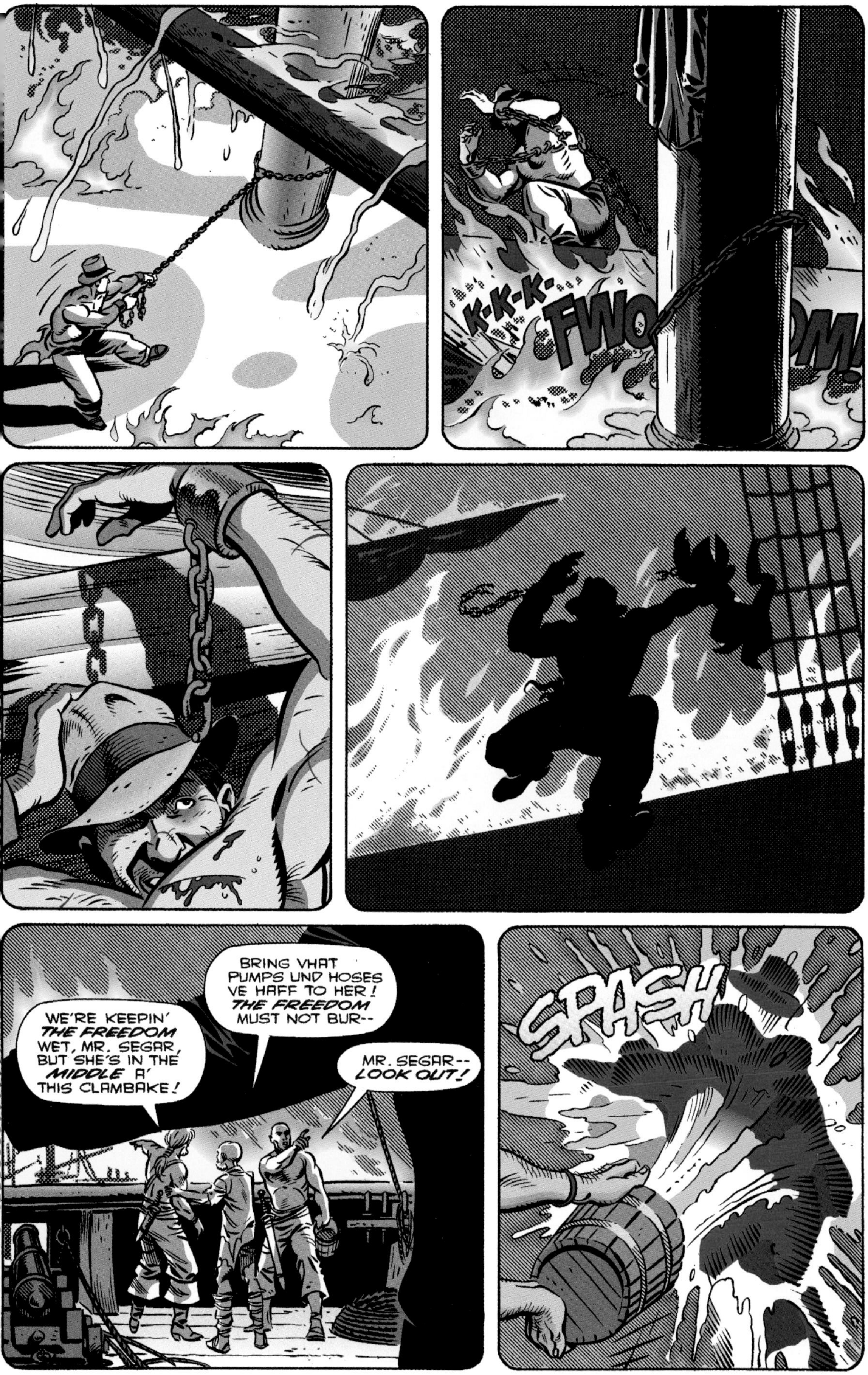

K-K-K-FWOOOM!
WE'RE KEEPIN' THE FREEDOM WET, MR. SEGAR, BUT SHE'S IN THE MIDDLE A' THIS CLAMBAKE!
BRING VHAT PUMPS UND HOSES VE HAFF TO HER! THE FREEDOM MUST NOT BUR--
MR. SEGAR-- LOOK OUT!
SPASH

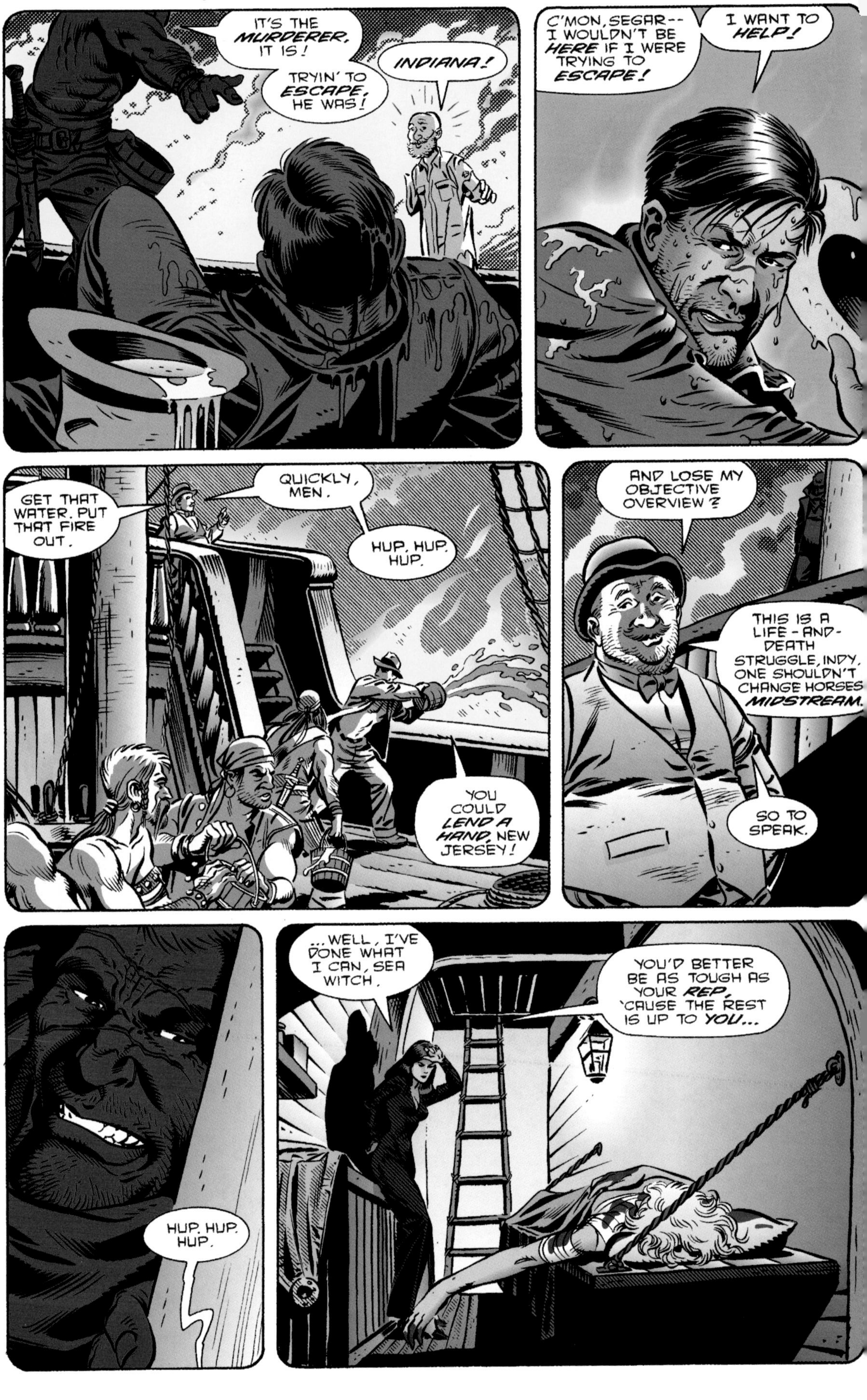
IT'S THE MURDERER, IT IS!
TRYIN' TO ESCAPE, HE WAS!
INDIANA!
C'MON, SEGAR-- I WOULDN'T BE HERE IF I WERE TRYING TO ESCAPE!
I WANT TO HELP!
GET THAT WATER. PUT THAT FIRE OUT.
QUICKLY, MEN.
HUP. HUP. HUP.
YOU COULD LEND A HAND, NEW JERSEY!
AND LOSE MY OBJECTIVE OVERVIEW?
THIS IS A LIFE-AND-DEATH STRUGGLE, INDY. ONE SHOULDN'T CHANGE HORSES MIDSTREAM.
SO TO SPEAK.
HUP. HUP. HUP.
...WELL, I'VE DONE WHAT I CAN, SEA WITCH.
YOU'D BETTER BE AS TOUGH AS YOUR REP, 'CAUSE THE REST IS UP TO YOU...

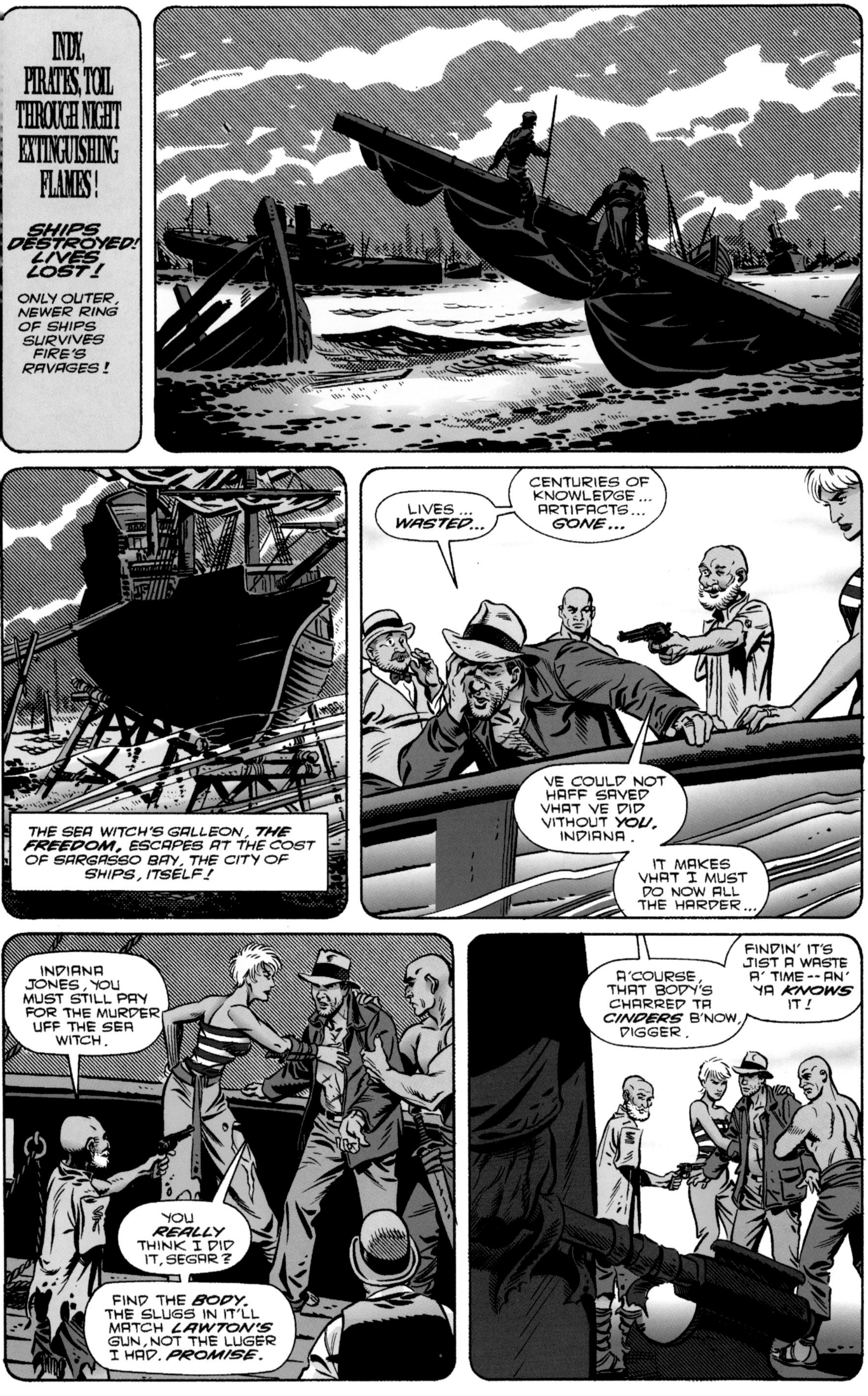
INDY, PIRATES, TOIL THROUGH NIGHT EXTINGUISHING FLAMES!
SHIPS DESTROYED! LIVES LOST!
ONLY OUTER, NEWER RING OF SHIPS SURVIVES FIRE'S RAVAGES!
THE SEA WITCH'S GALLEON, THE FREEDOM, ESCAPES AT THE COST OF SARGASSO BAY, THE CITY OF SHIPS, ITSELF!
LIVES... WASTED...
CENTURIES OF KNOWLEDGE... ARTIFACTS... GONE...
VE COULD NOT HAFF SAVED VHAT VE DID VITHOUT YOU, INDIANA.
IT MAKES VHAT I MUST DO NOW ALL THE HARDER...
INDIANA JONES, YOU MUST STILL PAY FOR THE MURDER UFF THE SEA WITCH.
YOU REALLY THINK I DID IT, SEGAR?
FIND THE BODY. THE SLUGS IN IT'LL MATCH LAWTON'S GUN, NOT THE LUGER I HAD. PROMISE.
A'COURSE, THAT BODY'S CHARRED TA CINDERS B'NOW, DIGGER.
FINDIN' IT'S JIST A WASTE A' TIME -- AN' YA KNOWS IT!

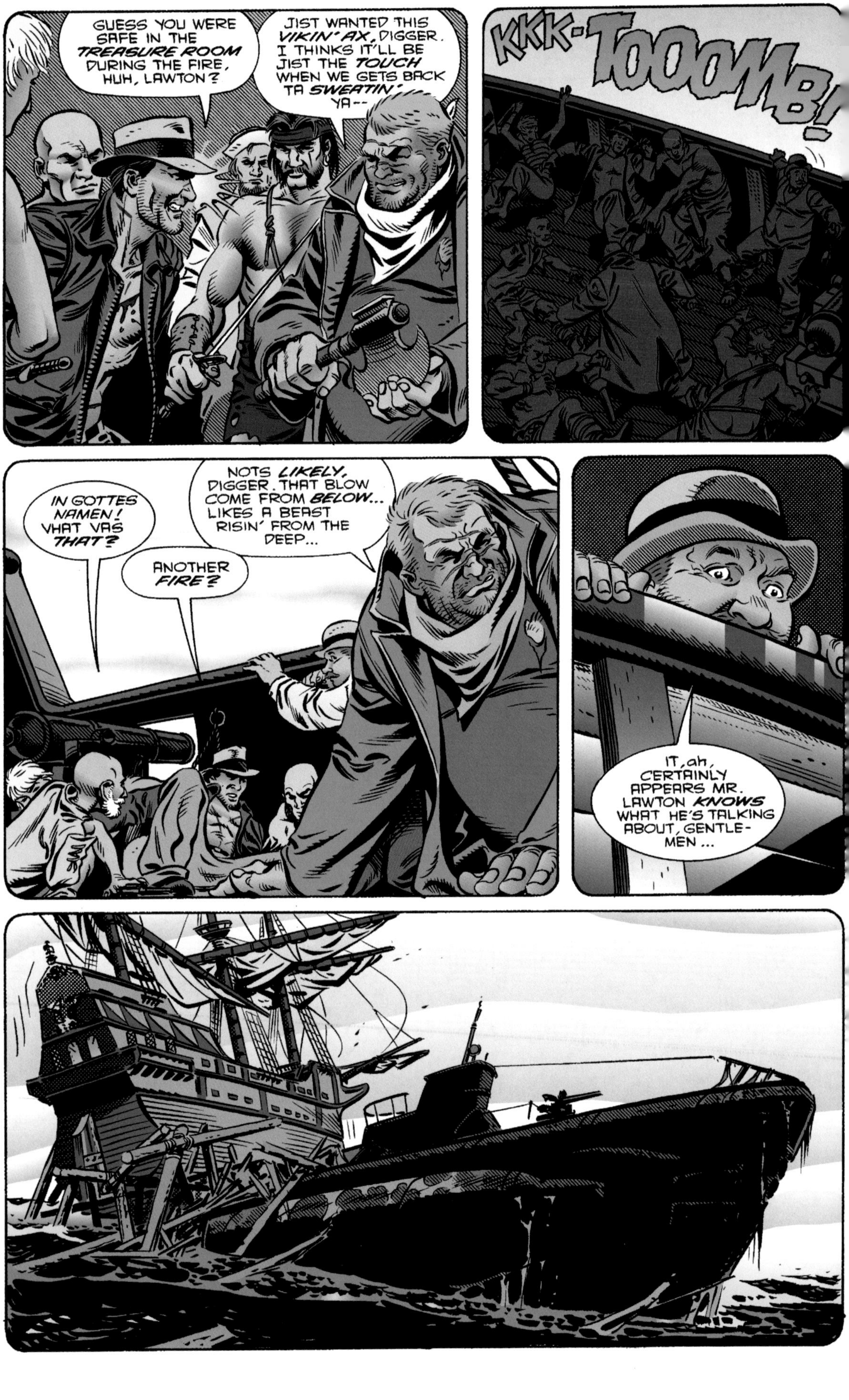
GUESS YOU WERE SAFE IN THE TREASURE ROOM DURING THE FIRE, HUH, LAWTON?
JIST WANTED THIS VIKIN' AX, DIGGER. I THINKS IT'LL BE JIST THE TOUCH WHEN WE GETS BACK TA SWEATIN' YA--
KKK-TOOOMB!
IN GOTTES NAMEN! VHAT VAS THAT?
ANOTHER FIRE?
NOTS LIKELY, DIGGER. THAT BLOW COME FROM BELOW... LIKES A BEAST RISIN' FROM THE DEEP...
IT, ah, CERTAINLY APPEARS MR. LAWTON KNOWS WHAT HE'S TALKING ABOUT, GENTLE-MEN ...

A SUBMARINE!

NEIN -- U-BOOT. VUN UFF THE GREY WOLVES I HAFF HEARD NEW VISITORS TALK ABOUT.

VERBLÜFFEND! SO MUCH LARGER THAN THE VUN I COMMANDED FOR DER KAISER...

PROBABLY GOT CAUGHT IN THE WEEDS TRYING TO SURFACE. THE FIRE MUST HAVE DESTROYED WHATEVER WAS KEEPING IT UNDER.

THINK ITS CREW'S ALIVE, SEGAR?

NEIN, INDY. NOT IF SHE VAS TRAPPED MORE THAN TWO DAYS.

JIST TELLS ME THIS, SEGAR -- CAN YA MAKES 'ER RUN?

I... I VOULD HAFF TO INSPECT HER, BUT... IF HER MOTORS UND HULL VERE INTACT ...IF HER ENGINEERING VAS NOT TOO ADVANCED...

...PERHAPS...

THAT'S ALL I NEEDS TA KNOW.

I GOTS A LI'L ANNOUNCEMENT TA MAKES ...

KEEPS THE DIGGER OUTTA TROUBLE, BULLY BOYS...

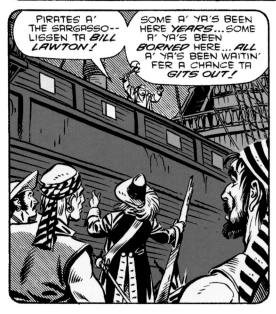

PIRATES A' THE SARGASSO -- LISSEN TA BILL LAWTON!

SOME A' YA'S BEEN HERE YEARS... SOME A' YA'S BEEN BORNED HERE... ALL A' YA'S BEEN WAITIN' FER A CHANCE TA GITS OUT!

WELL, YA GOTS THE CHANCE NOW! THAT THAR U-BOAT'LL DO THE TRICK!

NOW, I AIN'T SAYIN' IT'LL BE EASY -- BUT THEM WHAT HELPS SAILS OUT WITH ME!

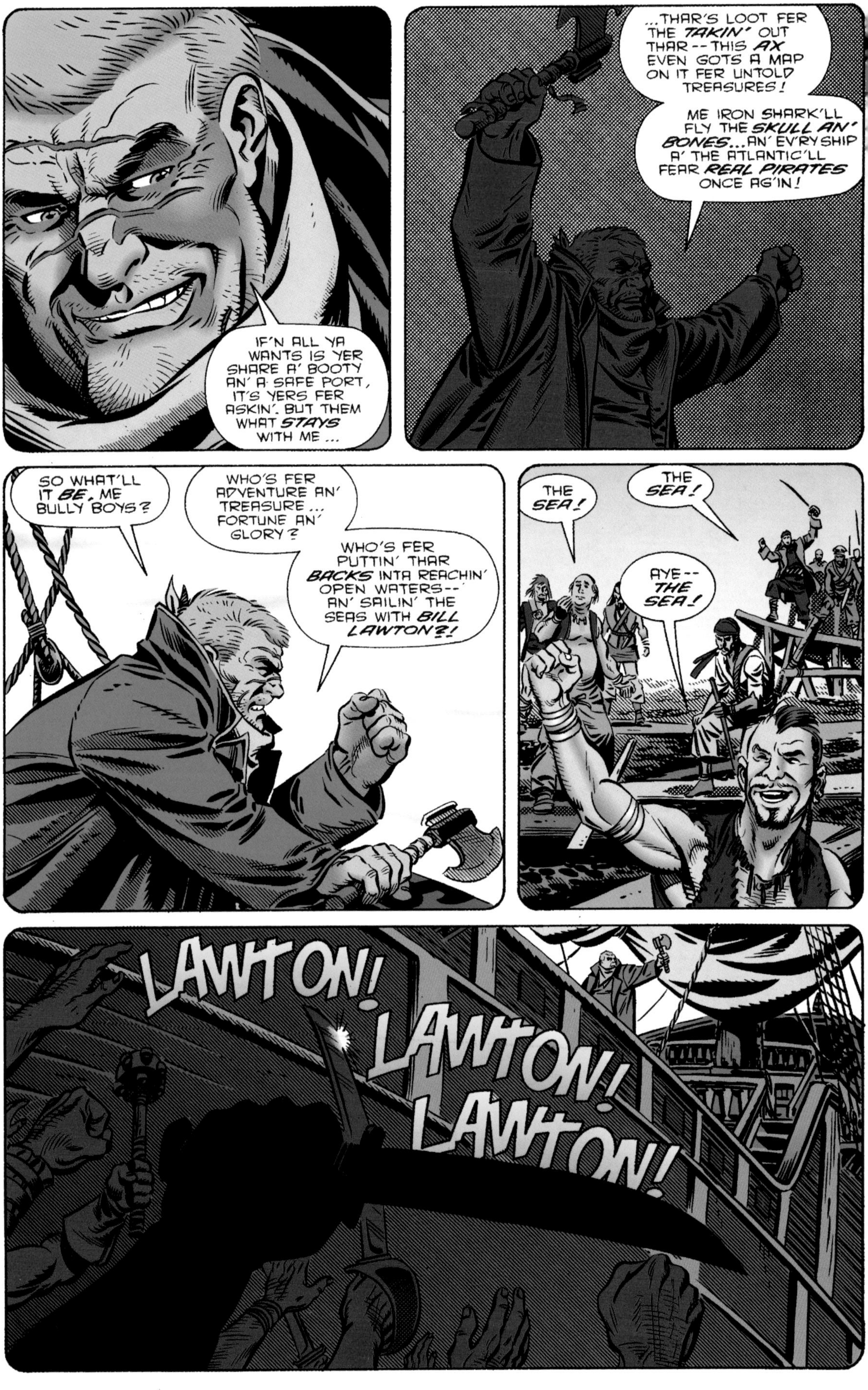
IF'N ALL YA WANTS IS YER SHARE A' BOOTY AN' A SAFE PORT, IT'S YERS FER ASKIN'. BUT THEM WHAT STAYS WITH ME ...
...THAR'S LOOT FER THE TAKIN' OUT THAR -- THIS AX EVEN GOTS A MAP ON IT FER UNTOLD TREASURES!
ME IRON SHARK'LL FLY THE SKULL AN' BONES...AN' EV'RYSHIP A' THE ATLANTIC'LL FEAR REAL PIRATES ONCE AG'IN!
SO WHAT'LL IT BE, ME BULLY BOYS?
WHO'S FER ADVENTURE AN' TREASURE... FORTUNE AN' GLORY?
WHO'S FER PUTTIN' THAR BACKS INTA REACHIN' OPEN WATERS-- AN' SAILIN' THE SEAS WITH BILL LAWTON?!
THE SEA!
THE SEA!
AYE -- THE SEA!
LAWTON!
LAWTON!
LAWTON!

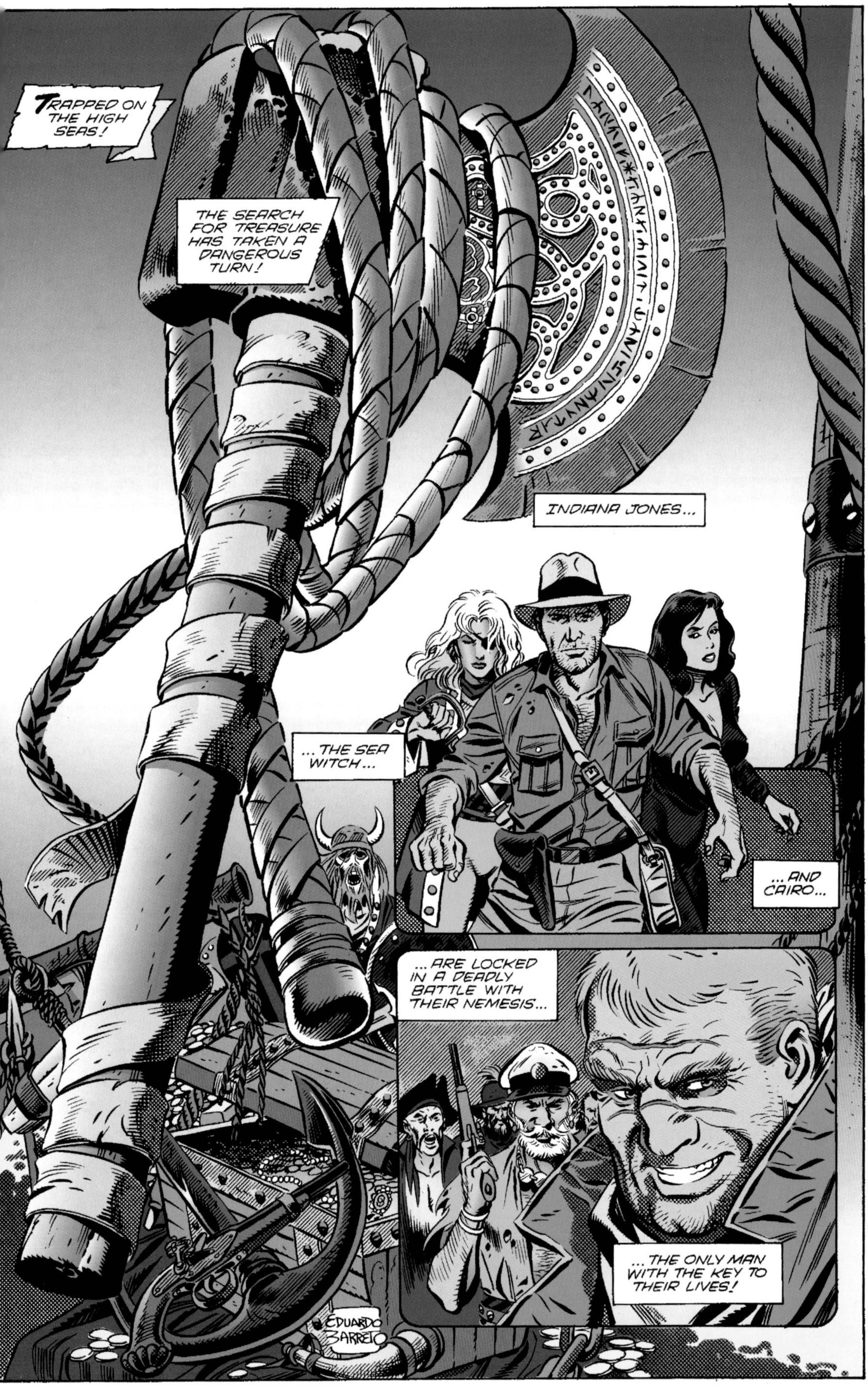
TRAPPED ON THE HIGH SEAS!
THE SEARCH FOR TREASURE HAS TAKEN A DANGEROUS TURN!
INDIANA JONES...
...THE SEA WITCH...
...AND CAIRO...
...ARE LOCKED IN A DEADLY BATTLE WITH THEIR NEMESIS...
...THE ONLY MAN WITH THE KEY TO THEIR LIVES!
EDUARDO BARRETO

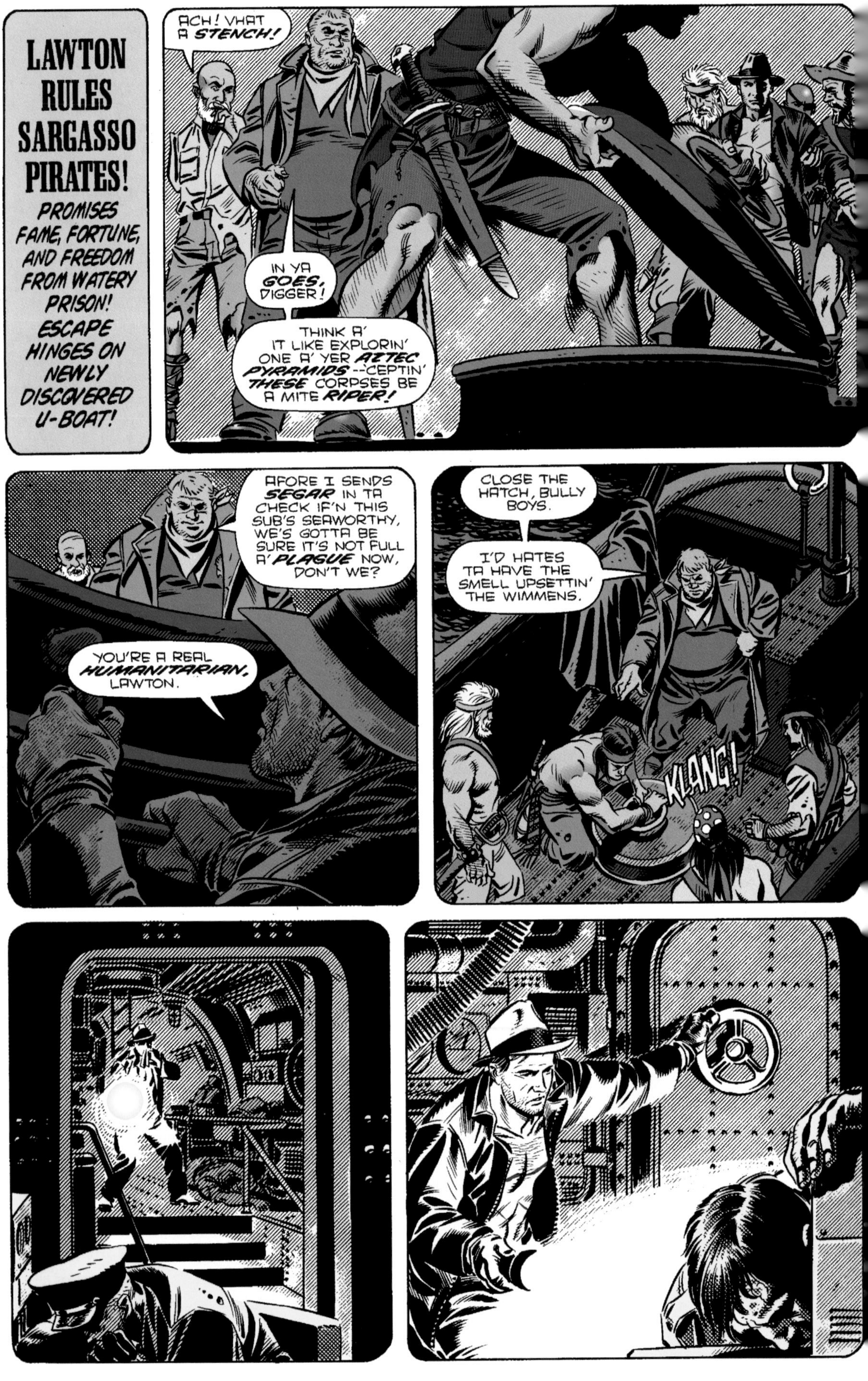
LAWTON RULES SARGASSO PIRATES!
PROMISES FAME, FORTUNE, AND FREEDOM FROM WATERY PRISON! ESCAPE HINGES ON NEWLY DISCOVERED U-BOAT!
ACH! VHAT A STENCH!
IN YA GOES, DIGGER!
THINK A' IT LIKE EXPLORIN' ONE A' YER AZTEC PYRAMIDS --'CEPTIN' THESE CORPSES BE A MITE RIPER!
AFORE I SENDS SEGAR IN TA CHECK IF'N THIS SUB'S SEAWORTHY, WE'S GOTTA BE SURE IT'S NOT FULL A' PLAGUE NOW, DON'T WE?
YOU'RE A REAL HUMANITARIAN, LAWTON.
CLOSE THE HATCH, BULLY BOYS.
I'D HATES TA HAVE THE SMELL UPSETTIN' THE WIMMENS.
KLANG!

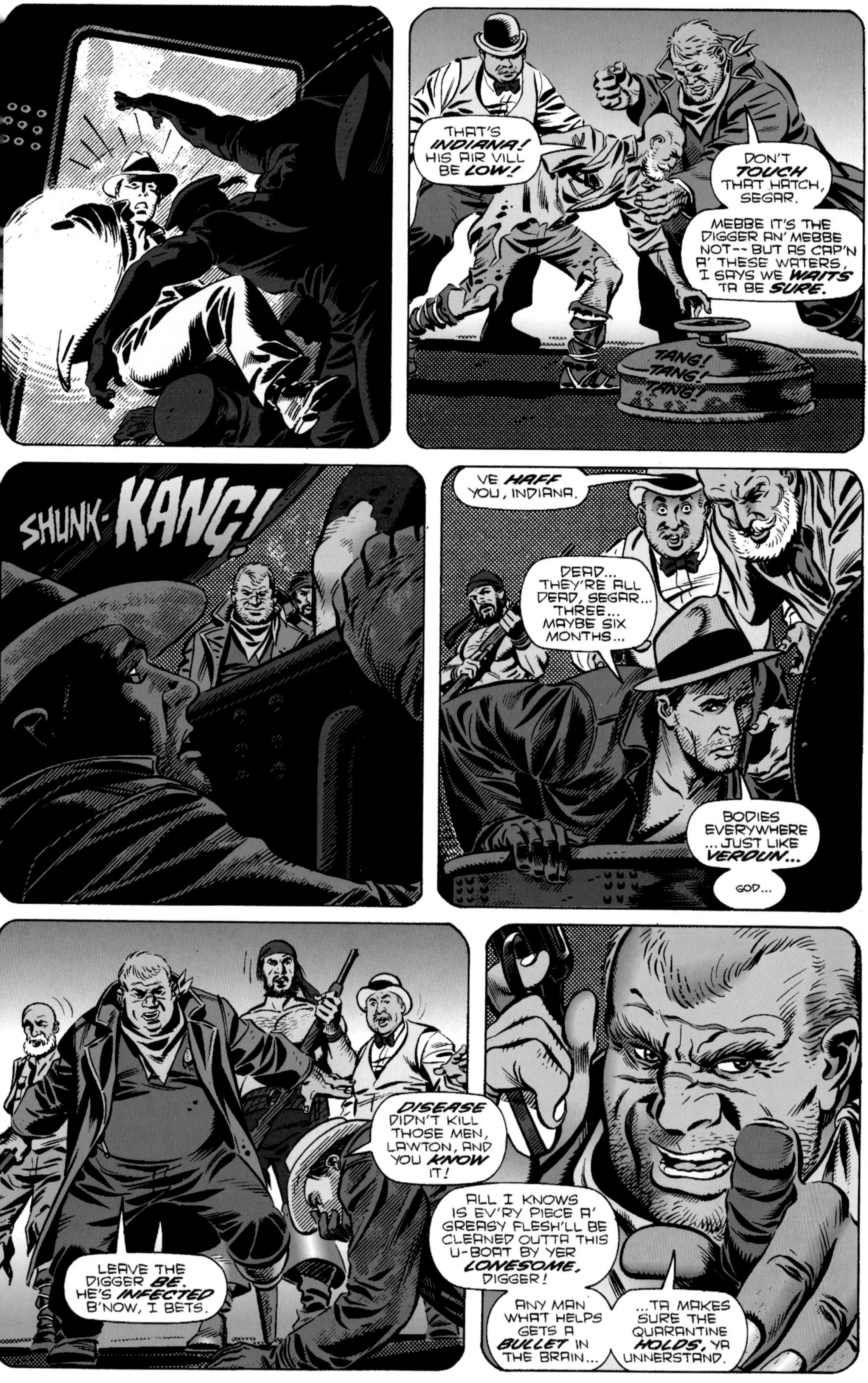

THAT'S INDIANA! HIS AIR VILL BE LOW!
DON'T TOUCH THAT HATCH, SEGAR.
MEBBE IT'S THE DIGGER AN' MEBBE NOT-- BUT AS CAP'N A' THESE WATERS, I SAYS WE WAITS TA BE SURE.
TANG! TANG! TANG!
SHUNK-KANG!
VE HAFF YOU, INDIANA.
DEAD... THEY'RE ALL DEAD, SEGAR... THREE... MAYBE SIX MONTHS...
BODIES EVERYWHERE ...JUST LIKE VERDUN...
GOD...
LEAVE THE DIGGER BE. HE'S INFECTED B'NOW, I BETS.
DISEASE DIDN'T KILL THOSE MEN, LAWTON, AND YOU KNOW IT!
ALL I KNOWS IS EV'RY PIECE A' GREASY FLESH'LL BE CLEANED OUTTA THIS U-BOAT BY YER LONESOME, DIGGER!
ANY MAN WHAT HELPS GETS A BULLET IN THE BRAIN...
...TA MAKES SURE THE QUARANTINE HOLDS, YA UNNERSTAND.

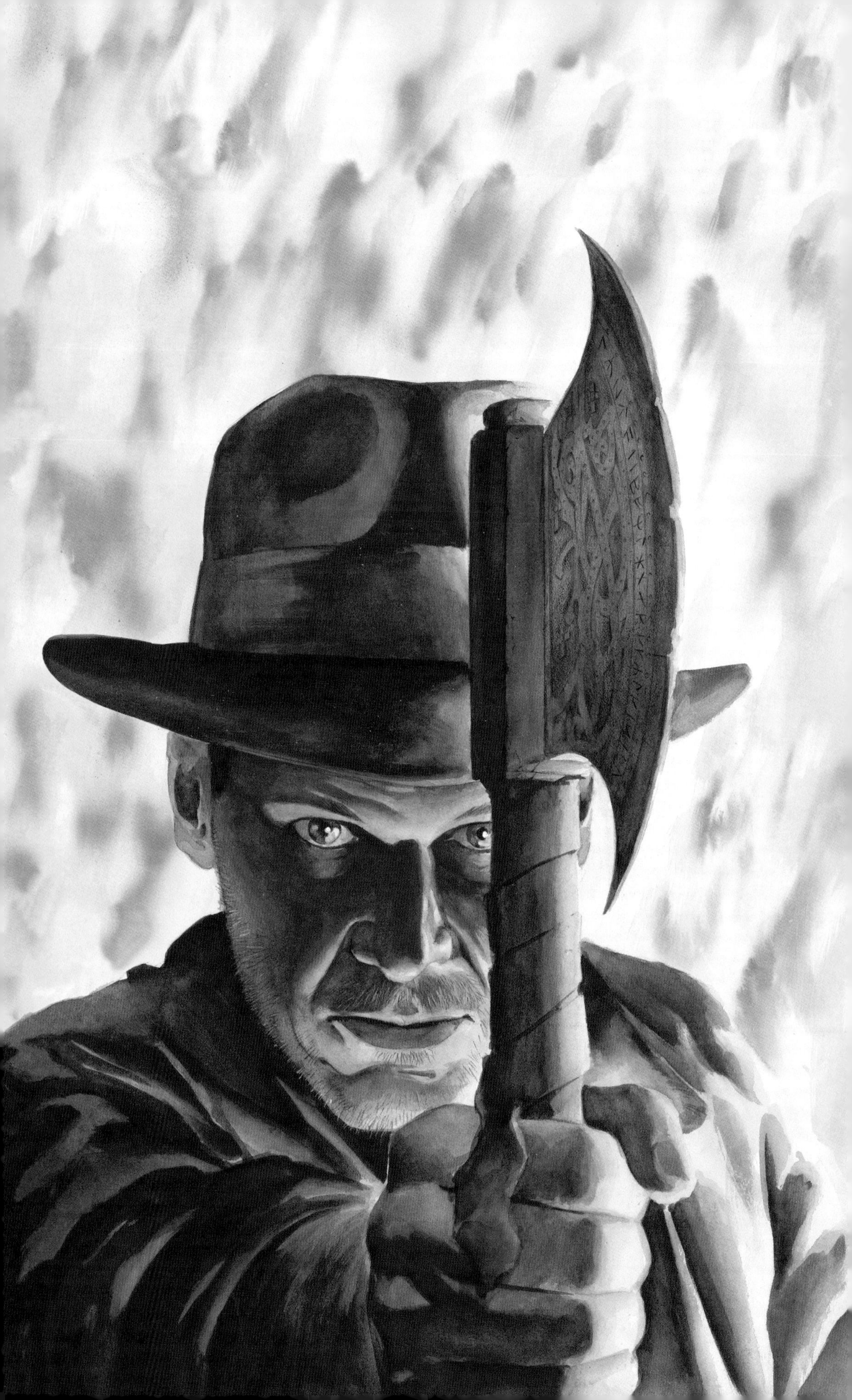

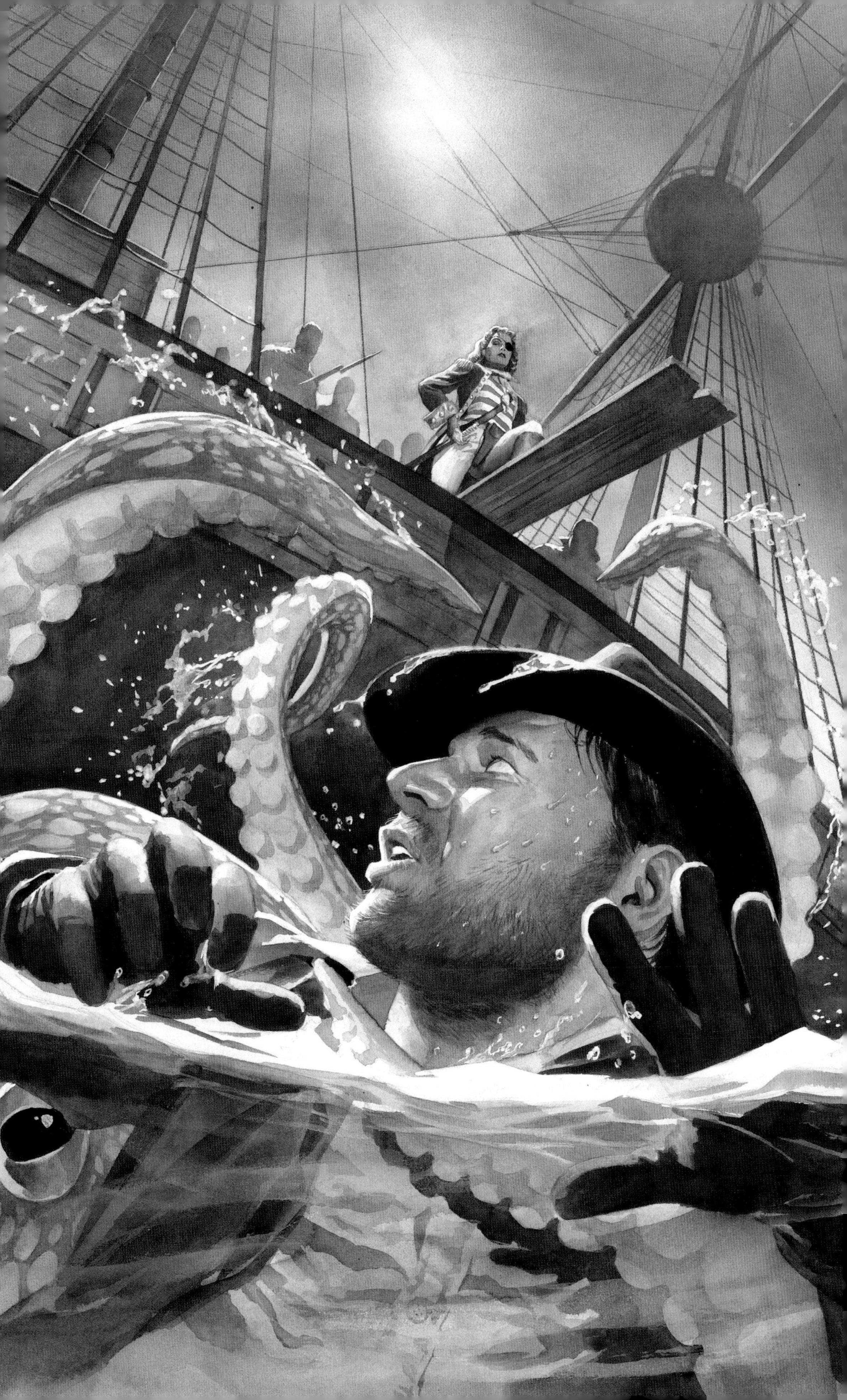

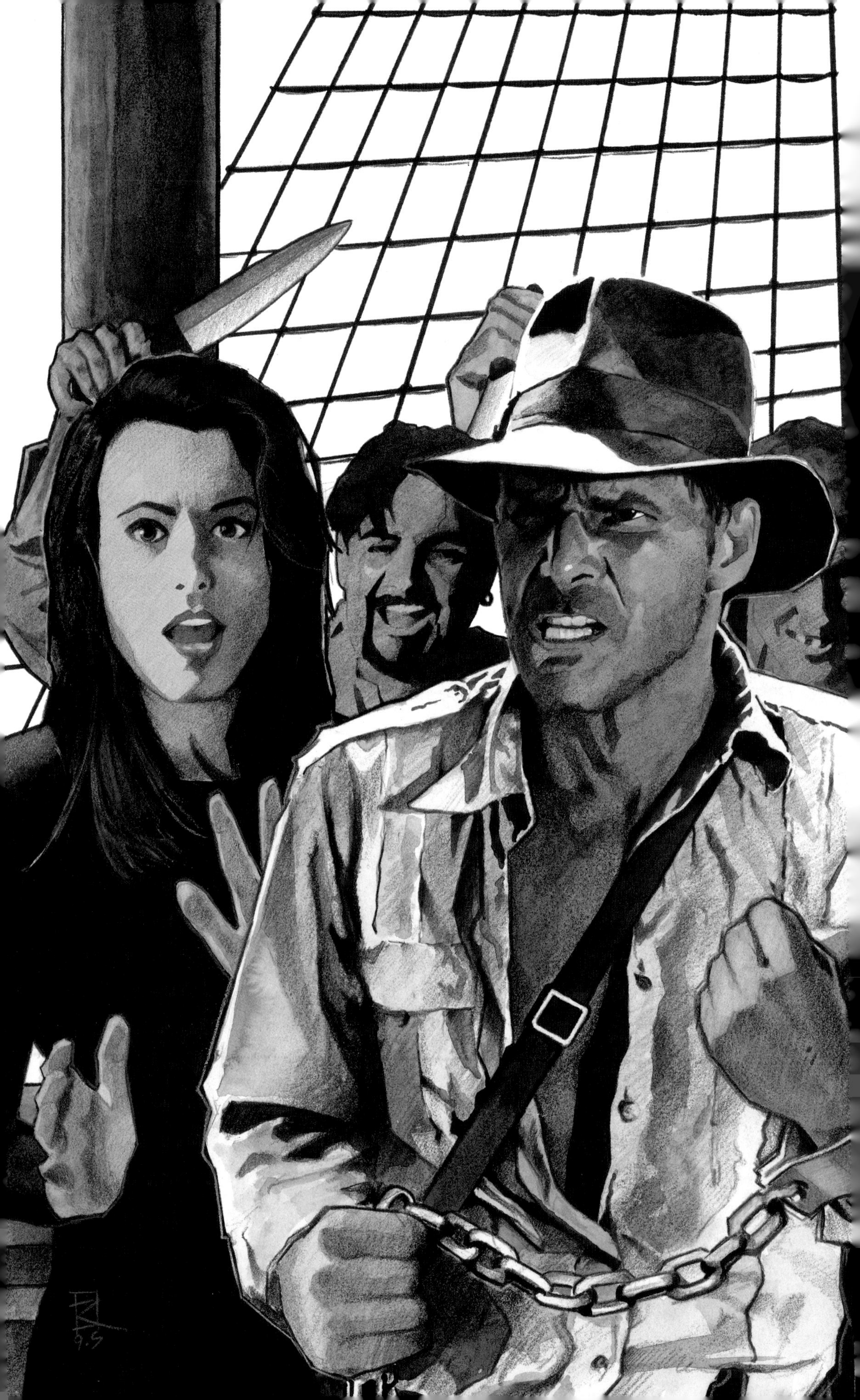